CHILDREN'S VERSE

Margaret Tarrant

CHILDREN'S VERSE

Margaret Tarrant

Salem House Publishers
Topsfield, Massachusetts

First published in the United States
by Salem House Publishers, 1986
462 Boston Street, Topsfield, MA 01983

ISBN: 0 88162 180 3

Printed and bound in Spain by Graficromo,
S.A., Cordoba

SING a song of sixpence,
    A pocket full of rye;
Four-and-twenty blackbirds
    Baked in a pie.

When the pie was opened,
    The birds began to sing;
Was not that a dainty dish
    To set before the King?

The King was in the counting-house,
    Counting out his money;
The Queen was in the parlour,
    Eating bread and honey;

The maid was in the garden,
    Hanging out the clothes;
When down came a little bird
    And snapped off her nose!

Little Boy Blue

LITTLE Boy Blue, come blow your horn!
   The sheep's in the meadow, the cow's in the corn.
Where's the boy that looks after the sheep?
   He's under the haycock, fast asleep.
Will you wake him? No, not I;
   For if I do, he'll be sure to cry.

The lobster

HE was a gentle lobster
  (The boats had just come in)–
He did not love the fishermen,
  He could not stand their din;
And so he quietly stole off,
  As if it were no sin.

She was a little maiden,
  He met her on the sand,
"And how d'you do?" the lobster said;
  "Why don't you give your hand?"
For why she edged away from him
  He *could* not understand.

"Excuse me, sir," the maiden said,
  "Excuse me, if you please,"
And put her hands behind her back,
  And doubled up her knees;
"I always thought that lobsters were
  A little apt to squeeze."
"Your ignorance," the lobster said,
  "Is natural, I fear;
Such scandal is a shame," he sobbed.
  "It is not true, my dear!"
And with his pocket handkerchief
  He wiped away a tear.

So out she put her little hand,
  As though she feared him not,
When someone grabbed him suddenly,
  And put him in a pot,
With water which, I think, he found
  Uncomfortably hot.

It may have been the water made
  The blood flow to his head,
It may have been that dreadful fib
  Lay on his soul like lead:
This much is true–he went in grey
  And came out very red.

There was an old woman who lived in a shoe

THERE was an old woman who lived in a shoe;
　　She had so many children she didn't know what to do.
She gave them some broth without any bread;
Then whipped them all soundly and put them to bed.

My shadow

I HAVE a little shadow, that goes in and out with me,
And what can be the use of him is more than I can see.
He is very, very like me from the heels up to the head;
And I see him jump before me when I jump into my bed.

The funniest thing about him is the way he likes to grow—
Not at all like proper children, which is always very slow;
But he sometimes shoots up taller, like an indiarubber ball,
And he sometimes gets so little that there's none of him at all.

He hasn't got a notion of how children ought to play,
And can only make a fool of me in every sort of way.
He stands so close beside me, he's a coward you can see;
I'd think shame to stick to nursie as that shadow sticks to me!

One morning, very early, before the sun was up,
I rose and found the shining dew on every buttercup;
But my lazy little shadow, like an arrant sleepy-head,
Had stayed at home behind me and was fast asleep in bed.

Ride a cock-horse to Banbury Cross

RIDE a cock-horse to Banbury Cross,
    To see a fine lady upon a white horse;
With rings on her fingers and bells on her toes
She shall have music wherever she goes.

A Chinese nursery song

THE mouse ran up the candlestick,
    To eat the grease from off the wick.
When he got up, he could not get down,
But squeaked to waken all the town:
Ma-ma-ma! Ma-ma-ma!

Three blind mice

THREE blind mice, three blind mice,
    See how they run! See how they run!
They all ran after the farmer's wife,
    Who cut off their tails with a carving knife.
Did ever you see such a thing in your life
    As three blind mice?

Baby, baby bunting

BABY, baby bunting,
Daddy's gone a-hunting,
To get a little rabbit's skin
To wrap his baby bunting in.

The Queen of Hearts

THE Queen of Hearts
She made some tarts
All on a summer's day;
The Knave of Hearts
He stole the tarts,
And with them ran away.
The King of Hearts
Called for the tarts,
And beat the Knave full sore;
The Knave of Hearts
Brought back the tarts,
And said he'd ne'er steal more.

Rub-a-dub-dub

Rub a dub dub,
    Three men in a tub;
And who do you think they be?
    The butcher, the baker,
The candlestick-maker;
    Turn 'em out, knaves all three!

Tartary

IF I were Lord of Tartary,
　　Myself and me alone,
My bed should be of ivory,
　　Of beaten gold my throne;
And in my court should peacocks flaunt,
And in my forests tigers haunt,
And in my pools great fishes slant
　　Their fins athwart the sun.

　　　　If I were Lord of Tartary,
　　　　　　Trumpeters every day
　　　　To all my meals should summon me,
　　　　　　And in my courtyards bray;
　　　　And in the evenings lamps should shine
　　　　Yellow as honey, red as wine,
　　　　While harp and flute and mandoline
　　　　　　Made music sweet and gay.

　　　　　　　　If I were Lord of Tartary,
　　　　　　　　　　I'd wear a robe of beads,
　　　　　　　　White, and gold, and green they'd be—
　　　　　　　　　　And small, and thick as seeds;
　　　　　　　　And ere should wane the morning star,
　　　　　　　　I'd don my robe and scimitar,
　　　　　　　　And zebras seven should draw my car
　　　　　　　　　　Through Tartary's dark glades.

　　　　　　　　　　Lord of the fruits of Tartary,
　　　　　　　　　　　　Her rivers silver-pale!
　　　　　　　　　　Lord of the hills of Tartary,
　　　　　　　　　　　　Glen, thicket, wood, and dale!
　　　　　　　　　　Her flashing stars, her scented breeze,
　　　　　　　　　　Her trembling lakes, like foamless seas,
　　　　　　　　　　Her bird-delighting citron-trees
　　　　　　　　　　　　In every purple vale!

Georgie Porgie

GEORGIE Porgie, pudding and pie,
    Kiss'd the girls and made them cry;
When the girls came out to play
Georgie Porgie ran away.

Mary, Mary, quite contrary

MARY, Mary, quite contrary,
How does your garden grow?
With cockle shells and silver bells
And cowslips all in a row.

The pedlar's caravan

I WISH I lived in a caravan,
  With a horse to drive, like a pedlar-man!
Where he comes from nobody knows,
  Or where he goes to, but on he goes!

His caravan has windows two,
    And a chimney of tin, that the smoke
        comes through;
He has a wife with a baby brown,
    And they go a-riding from town to town.

    The roads are brown, and the sea is green,
        But his house is like a bathing-machine;
    The world is round, and he can ride,
        Rumble and splash, to the other side!

    Chairs to mend, and delf to sell!
        He clashes the basins like a bell;
    Tea-trays, baskets ranged in order,
        Plates, with alphabets round the border!

        With the pedlar-man I should like to roam,
            And write a book when I came home;
        All the people would read my book,
            Just like the Travels of Captain Cook!

Night and day

WHEN the golden day is done,
   Through the closing portal,
Child and garden, flower and sun,
   Vanish all things mortal.

As the blinding shadows fall,
   . As the rays diminish,
Under evening's cloak they all
   Roll away and finish.

Garden darkened, daisy shut,
   Child in bed, they slumber–
Glow-worm in the highway rut,
   Mice among the lumber.

In the darkness houses shine,
   Parents move with candles,
Till on all, the night divine
   Turns the bedroom handles.

Till at last the day begins
   In the east a-breaking,
In the hedges and the whins
   Sleeping birds a-waking.

In the darkness shapes of things,
   Houses, trees, and hedges,
Clearer grow, and sparrows' wings
   Beat on window ledges.

These shall wake the yawning maid;
   She the door shall open–
Finding dew on garden glade
   And the morning broken.

There my garden grows again
   Green and rosy painted,
As at eve behind the pane
   From my eyes it fainted.

Just as it was shut away,
   Toy-like, in the even,
Here I see it glow with day
   Under glowing heaven.

Every path and every plot,
  Every bush of roses,
Every blue forget-me-not
  Where the dew reposes—

"Up!" they cry, "the day is come
  On the smiling valleys;
We have beat the morning drum,
  Playmate, join your allies!"

The bee

THERE is a little gentleman
  That wears the yellow trews,
A dirk below his doublet,
  For sticking of his foes.

He's in a stinging posture
  Where'er you do him see,
And if you offer violence
  He'll stab his dirk in thee.

Twinkle, twinkle, little star

TWINKLE, twinkle, little star,
How I wonder what you are!
Up above the world so high
Like a diamond in the sky!

When the blazing sun is gone,
When he nothing shines upon,
Then you show your little light—
Twinkle, twinkle, all the night.

Then the traveller in the dark
Thanks you for your little spark!
He could not tell which way to go
If you did not twinkle so.

In the dark blue sky you keep,
While you through my curtains peep;
And you never shut your eye
Till the sun is in the sky.

The old man in the moon

"SAY, where have you been, Frank—say, where have you been?"
    "Oh! I've been a long way: I've been to the moon."
"But how did you get there? and what have you seen?"
    "Oh! I went, to be sure, in my little balloon.

    "And I've seen—why, I've seen the old man who lives there;
        And his mouth, it grew bigger the nearer I got;
    So I pulled off my hat, made a bow with an air,
        And said, 'Sir, you inhabit a very bright spot.'

        "And the old man he laughed, he laughed long and loud;
            And he patted my cheek as he graciously said,
        'You had better return, nor get lost in a cloud;
            And besides, it is time that we both were in bed.'"

Little Miss Muffet

LITTLE Miss Muffet sat on a tuffet,
  Eating her curds and whey;
There came a great spider and sat down beside her,
And frightened Miss Muffet away.

Pat-a-cake, pat-a-cake

PAT-a-cake, pat-a-cake, baker's man!
Make me a cake as fast as you can;
Pat it, and prick it, and mark it with B,
Put it in the oven for Baby and me.

Sing a song of morning

SING a song of morning,
 Sunshine bright outside,
Roses at the window,
 Blue eyes opening wide,
Sound of water splashing,
 Hair well brushed and neat,
Breakfast on the table,
 Mother's smile so sweet.

Sing a song of schooltime,
 Fun the road along,
Merry comrades marching
 All in time to song,
Teacher's kindly greeting,
 Work well done, sums right,
Every scholar's motto,
 "Try with all your might."

Sing a song of evening,
 Birds that homeward fly,
Roses pale as silver
 'Neath the twilight sky,
Little prayers low whispered,
 Heads on pillows white,
Kisses for dear mother—
 Sleep till morning's light.

29

Ding, dong, bell

DING, dong, bell,
  Pussy's in the well.
Who put her in?
  Little Tommy Green.
Who pulled her out?
  Little Tommy Stout.
What a naughty boy was that
  To drown poor pussy cat,
Who never did him any harm,
  But killed the mice in father's barn.

A pattern baby

WHEN people come to call and tell
 About their babies, dear me, well–
  I sit and listen all the while
  And smile myself a little smile.
If mine were like some people's, there,
I would not keep her, I declare!

 Their babies scream and cry and fret,
 Won't eat or sleep, while my dear pet

  She *never* cries; she'll stay for hours
  Just looking at the birds and flowers.

The sweetest little cot has she,
All pink and white, as smart can be.
 And when at night I lay her in it
 She shuts her eyes in half a minute.

 That all the babies in the city
 Are not like mine I think a pity.
 The only thing is, mine won't grow–
 She is a baby doll, you know.

Once I saw a little boat

ONCE I saw a little boat, and a pretty, pretty boat,
    When daybreak the hills was adorning,
And into it I jumped, and away I did float,
    So very, very early in the morning.

        For every little wave has its nightcap on,
            Its nightcap, white cap, nightcap on,
        For every little wave has its nightcap on,
            So very, very early in the morning.

All the fishes were asleep in their caves cool and deep,
    When the ripple round my keel flashed a warning;
Said the minnow to the skate, "We must certainly be late
    Though I thought 'twas very early in the morning."

        For every little wave has its nightcap on,
            Its nightcap, white cap, nightcap on,
        For every little wave has its nightcap on,
            So very, very early in the morning.

The lobster, darkly green, soon appeared upon the scene,
    And pearly drops his claws were adorning;
Quoth he, "May I be boiled if I'll have my pleasure spoiled
    So very, very early in the morning!"

        For every little wave has its nightcap on,
            Its nightcap, white cap, nightcap on,
        For every little wave has its nightcap on,
            So very, very early in the morning.

Said the sturgeon to the eel, "Just imagine how I feel,
    Thus roused without a syllable of warning;
People ought to let us know when a-sailing they would go
    So very, very early in the morning."

        When every little wave has its nightcap on,
            Its nightcap, white cap, nightcap on,
        When every little wave has its nightcap on,
            So very, very early in the morning.

Just then, up jumped the sun, and the fishes every one
    For their laziness at once fell a-mourning.
But I stayed to hear no more, for my boat had reached the
        shore,
    So very, very early in the morning.

And every little wave took its nightcap off,
Its nightcap, white cap, nightcap off,
And every little wave took its nightcap off,
And curtsied to the sun in the morning.

Humpty Dumpty

HUMPTY Dumpty sat on a wall,
    Humpty Dumpty had a great fall;
Not all the king's horses, nor all the king's men
Could set Humpty Dumpty together again.

Autumn fires

IN the other gardens
And all up the vale,
From the autumn bonfires
See the smoke trail!

Pleasant summer over
And all the summer flowers,
The red fire blazes,
The grey smoke towers.

Sing a song of seasons!
Something bright in all!
Flowers in the summer,
Fires in the fall!

Our cat

OH, I wish that you had seen him,
　　Our little pussy-cat,
He came so skinny, scrag, and lean,
　　And went away so fat.
They said he stole the food and things,
　　Perhaps he did so, but,
He really couldn't help it,
　　　　　　Couldn't Smut.

He walked upon the dresser-shelf,
　　And knocked down mother's jugs;
Broke half-a-dozen dinner plates,
　　And Kate's and Molly's mugs.
I guess he thought he heard a mouse;
　　He did not catch it, but,
He really couldn't help it,
　　　　　　Couldn't Smut.

At night he went upon the spree.
　　And danced upon the tiles,
His caterwaul re-echoing round,
　　For miles, and miles, and miles.
Poor Pater said it woke him up,
　　No doubt it did so, but,
He really couldn't help it,
　　　　　　Couldn't Smut.

He tore up half the leather chairs,
　　They bought a set to match,
And just to show he noticed it,
　　He marked them with a scratch.
Then Pater he was raging mad;
　　It was annoying, but,
He really couldn't help it,
　　　　　　Couldn't Smut.

So of fellowship and feelings too,
　　We made a sacrifice,
And gave him to a farmer-man,
　　To catch his rats and mice.
We wept to lose our pussy-cat,
　　And he was sorry, but,
We really couldn't help it,
　　　　　　Could we, Smut?

Ring-a-ring of roses

Ring-a-ring of roses,
    A pocket full of posies.
Tishoo! Tishoo!
We all fall down.

Where are you going to, my pretty maid?

"WHERE are you going to, my pretty maid?"
"I'm going a-milking, sir," she said.

"May I go with you, my pretty maid?"
"You're kindly welcome, sir," she said.

"What is your father, my pretty maid?"
"My father's a farmer, sir," she said.

"What is your fortune, my pretty maid?"
"My face is my fortune, sir," she said.

"Then I can't marry you, my pretty maid!"
"Nobody asked you, sir!" she said.

Little Jack Horner

LITTLE Jack Horner
Sat in a corner,
Eating a Christmas pie;
He put in his thumb,
And pulled out a plum,
And cried "What a good boy am I!"

The first of June

THE wind to west is steady,
  The weather is sweet and fair;
Laburnum, slender lady,
  Shakes out her yellow hair.

Magnolia, like a stranger,
  Stands stiffly all alone;
I think a word would change her
  Into a flower of stone.

The solid guelder roses
  Are white as dairy cream;
The hyacinths fade, like posies;
  The cloud hangs in a dream.

And dreams of light and shadow
  The sleeping meadow shake,
But the king-cup shines in the meadow,
  A gold eye wide awake.

Old King Cole

OLD King Cole was a merry old soul,
   And a merry old soul was he;
He called for his pipe, he called for his glass,
And he called for his fiddlers three.

Every fiddler he had a fine fiddle,
And a very fine fiddle had he;
Twee-tweedle-dee, tweedle-dee, went the fiddlers.
Oh, there's none so rare as can compare
With King Cole and his fiddlers three!

Hey, Diddle, Diddle

HEY, Diddle, Diddle, the cat and the fiddle,
    The cow jumped over the moon,
The little dog laughed to see such fun,
    And the dish ran away with the spoon.

Come unto these yellow sands

COME unto these yellow sands,
   And then take hands:
Curtsied when you have and kiss'd,
The wild waves whist,
Foot it featly here and there;
And, sweet sprites, the burden bear.
Hark, hark!
Bow-wow
The watch-dogs bark:
Bow-wow.
Hark, hark! I hear
The strain of strutting chanticleer
Cry, Cock-a-diddle-dow.

Jack Sprat

JACK Sprat could eat no fat,
His wife could eat no lean;
And so betwixt them both, you see,
They lick'd the platter clean.

An American Indian lullaby

LULLABY, baby-bunting
Lullaby, by-by.
Baby bunting—
Baby bunting—
Lullaby.

Jack and Jill

JACK and Jill went up the hill
  To fetch a pail of water;
Jack fell down and cracked his crown,
  And Jill came tumbling after.

Then up Jack got, and home did trot,
  As fast as he could caper.
They put him to bed and plastered his head
  With vinegar and brown paper.

Little Bo-peep

LITTLE Bo-peep has lost her sheep,
    And can't tell where to find them;
Leave them alone and they'll come home,
    And bring their tails behind them.

        Little Bo-peep fell fast asleep,
            And dreamt she heard them bleating;
        But when she awoke, she found it a joke,
            For they were still a-fleeting.

Then up she took her little crook,
    Determined for to find them;
She found them indeed, but it made her heart bleed,
    For they'd left their tails behind them.

        It happened one day, as Bo-peep did stray
            Over a meadow hard by,
        That there she espied their tails side by side,
            All hung on a tree to dry.

She heaved a sigh, and gave by and by
    Each careless sheep a banging;
And as for the rest, she thought it was best
    Just to leave the tails a-hanging.

The Rock-a-by Lady

THE Rock-a-by Lady from Hushaby Street
   Comes stealing; comes creeping;
The poppies they hang from her head to her feet,
And each hath a dream that is tiny and fleet—
She bringeth her poppies to you, my sweet,
   When she findeth you sleeping!

There is one little dream of a beautiful drum—
   "Rub-a-dub!" it goeth;
There is one little dream of a big sugar-plum,
And lo! thick and fast the other dreams come
Of pop-guns that bang, and tin tops that hum,
   And a trumpet that bloweth!

And dollies peep out of those wee little dreams
   With laughter and singing;
And boats go a-floating on silvery streams,
And the stars peek-a-boo with their own misty gleams,
And up, up, and up, where the Mother Moon beams,
   The fairies go winging!

Would you dream all these dreams that are tiny and fleet?
   They'll come to you sleeping;
So shut the two eyes that are weary, my sweet,
For the Rock-a-by Lady from Hushaby Street,
With poppies that hang from her head to her feet,
   Comes stealing; comes creeping.

A boy's song

WHERE the pools are bright and deep,
   Where the grey trout lies asleep,
Up the river and over the lea,
   That's the way for Billy and me.

   Where the blackbird sings the latest,
      Where the hawthorn blooms the sweetest,
   Where the nestlings chirp and flee,
      That's the way for Billy and me.

Where the mowers mow the cleanest,
   Where the hay lies thick and greenest,
There to track the homeward bee,
   That's the way for Billy and me.

   Where the hazel bank is steepest,
      Where the shadow falls the deepest,
   Where the clustering nuts fall free,
      That's the way for Billy and me.

Why the boys should drive away
   Little sweet maidens from the play,
Or love to banter and fight so well,
   That's the thing I never could tell.

   But this I know, I love to play
      Through the meadow, among the hay;
   Up the water and over the lea,
      That's the way for Billy and me.

Polly, put the kettle on

POLLY, put the kettle on,
   Polly, put the kettle on,
Polly, put the kettle on,
   We'll all have tea.

Sukey, take it off again,
   Sukey, take it off again,
Sukey, take it off again,
   They've all gone away.

Oxfordshire children's May song

SPRING is coming, spring is coming,
   Birdies, build your nest;
Weave together straw and feather,
   Doing each your best.

Spring is coming, spring is coming,
   All around is fair:
Shimmer and quiver on the river,
   Joy is everywhere.

Spring is coming, spring is coming,
   Flowers are coming too:
Pansies, lilies, daffodillies
   Now are coming through.

We wish you a happy May.

Hush-a-bye, Baby

HUSH-a-bye, Baby, on the tree top,
   When the wind blows the cradle will rock;
When the bough breaks the cradle will fall,
Down will come baby, and cradle, and all.

Old Mother Hubbard

OLD Mother Hubbard she went to the cupboard
To get her poor dog a bone,
But when she got there the cupboard was bare,
And so the poor dog had none.

She went to the baker's
To buy him some bread;
But when she came back
The poor dog was dead.

She took a clean dish
To get him some tripe;
But when she came back
He was smoking a pipe.

She went to the tavern
For white wine and red;
But when she came back
The dog stood on his head.

She went to the barber's
To buy him a wig;
But when she came back
He was dancing a jig.

She went to the tailor's
To buy him a coat;
But when she came back
He was riding a goat.

She went to the joiner's
To buy him a coffin;
But when she came back
The poor dog was laughing.

She went to the fishmonger's
To buy him some fish;
And when she came back
He was licking the dish.

She went to the hatter's
To buy him a hat;
But when she came back
He was feeding the cat.

She went to the cobbler's
To buy him some shoes;
But when she came back
He was reading the news.

She went to the fruiterer's
  To buy him some fruit;
But when she came back
  He was playing the flute.

She went to the seamstress
  To buy him some linen;
But when she came back
  The dog was spinning.

The dame made a curtsy,
  The dog made a bow;
The dame said, "Your servant,"
  The dog said, "Bow, wow!"

The land of story books

AT evening when the lamp is lit,
  Around the fire my parents sit;
They sit at home and talk and sing,
  And do not play at anything.

  Now, with my little gun, I crawl
    All in the dark along the wall,
  And follow round the forest track
    Away behind the sofa back.

    There, in the night, where none can spy,
      All in my hunter's camp I lie,
    And play at books that I have read
      Till it is time to go to bed.

      These are the hills, these are the woods,
        These are my starry solitudes;
      And there the river by whose brink,
        The roaring lions come to drink.

        I see the others far away
          As if in firelit camp they lay,
        And I, like to an Indian scout,
          Around their party prowled about.

So, when my nurse comes in for me,
Home I return across the sea,
And go to bed with backward looks
At my dear land of story books.

Wee Willie Winkie

WEE Willie Winkie runs through the town,
    Upstairs and downstairs in his night-gown,
Tapping at the window, crying through the lock,
"Are the babes in their beds,
    For it's now ten o'clock?"

"Hey! Willie Winkie,
Are you coming then?
The cat's singing purrie
To the sleeping hen;
The dog is lying on the floor
And does not even peep;
But here's a wakeful laddie
That will not fall asleep.

"Anything but sleep, you rogue!
Glowering like the moon;
Rattling in an iron jug
With an iron spoon;
Rumbling, tumbling all about,
Crowing like a cock,
Screaming like I don't know what,
Waking sleeping folk.

"Hey! Willie Winkie,
Can't you keep him still?
Wriggling off a body's knee
Like a very eel;
Pulling at the cat's ear,
As she drowsy hums—
Hey, Willie Winkie!
See!—there he comes!"

Wearied is the mother
That has a restless wean,
A wee, stumpy bairnie,
Heard whene'er he's seen—
That has a battle aye with sleep
Before he'll close an e'e;
But a kiss from off his rosy lips
Gives strength anew to me.

Little Tom Tucker

LITTLE Tom Tucker, sing for your supper.
What shall he sing for? White bread and butter.
How shall he cut it without any knife?
How shall he marry without any wife?

Index of first lines